MONSIEUR SAGUETTE

AND HIS BAGUETTE

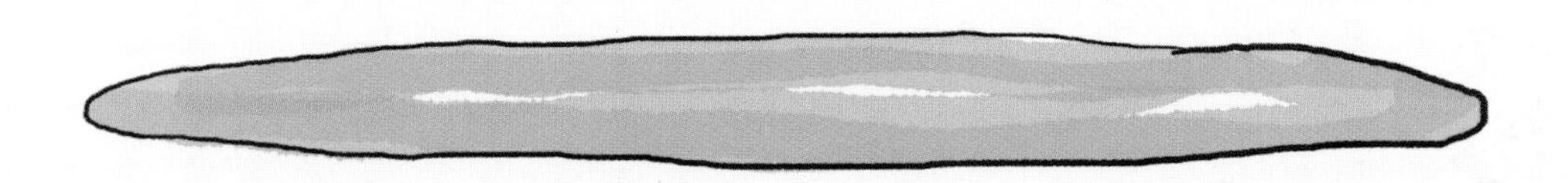

Frank Asch

KIDS CAN PRESS

Kids Can Press acknowledges the financial support of the Government of Ontario, through the Ontario Media Development Corporation's Ontario Book Initiative, and the Government of Canada, through the BPIDP, for our publishing activity.

Published in Canada by
Kids Can Press Ltd.
29 Birch Avenue
Toronto, ON M4V 1E2

Published in the U.S. by
Kids Can Press Ltd.
2250 Military Road
Tonawanda, NY 14150

www.kidscanpress.com

The artwork in this book was created in Photoshop.
The text is set in Alghera.

Edited by Tara Walker
Designed by Karen Powers
Printed and bound in Hong Kong, China, by Book Art Inc., Toronto
This book is smyth sewn casebound.

CM 04 0 9 8 7 6 5 4 3 2 1

National Library of Canada Cataloguing in Publication Data

Asch, Frank
Monsieur Saguette and his baguette / Frank Asch.

ISBN 1-55337-461-4

I. Title.

PZ7.A778 Mon 2003 j813'.54 C2002-902602-4

Kids Can Press is a Corus™ Entertainment company

To our gracious SERVAS hosts,
Maria Elena and Jean-Pierre
and their adorable children

One Sunday afternoon Monsieur Saguette made himself a pot of hot carrot soup.

"Ah, soup and bread," he said, smacking his lips. "My favorite!"

La Boulangerie

But there was no bread in Monsieur Saguette's house.

"What a nuisance!" he thought, and he walked to the bakery to buy himself a baguette.

On his way home Monsieur Saguette came upon a little girl who was crying.

"Why are you crying?" he asked.

"Because my cat climbed a tree and can't get down," sobbed the little girl.

"Don't worry," said Monsieur Saguette, and he held his baguette up to the tree so the cat could climb down.

"Thank you!" said the little girl.

"You're welcome," said Monsieur Saguette.

"Meow!" said the cat.

As Monsieur Saguette continued on his way home he came upon a chilling sight. An alligator had escaped from the zoo and was about to eat a baby ...

"Help! Help!" cried the baby's mother.

"Fear not!" declared Monsieur Saguette, and he wedged his baguette in the alligator's open jaws.

"My hero!" said the mother.
"It was nothing," said Monsieur Saguette.
"Goo goo," said the baby.

A little way down the block Monsieur Saguette came upon a marching band. But none of the musicians were marching or making any music.

"What's the problem?" Monsieur Saguette asked a little boy.

"The bandleader lost his baton," replied the boy.

"What a *shame*," said Monsieur Saguette, and he offered his baguette to the bandleader.

"I've never conducted with a baguette before," said the bandleader. "But I'll give it a try."

"Good luck," said Monsieur Saguette.

"Hip, hip, hooray!" cheered the musicians.

And the parade was a grand *success*!

As Monsieur Saguette walked along the river after the parade, he came upon a man about to be robbed.

"Drop your gun!" said Monsieur Saguette, and he stuck his baguette in the robber's back.

"Please, don't shoot," begged the robber. "I give up!"

Armed with only his baguette, Monsieur Saguette held the robber at bay until a policeman arrived.

"Good work!" said the officer.

"Just trying to help," said Monsieur Saguette.

"I want to talk to my lawyer," said the robber.

ATTENTION

Now Monsieur Saguette was almost home. But as he stepped off the curb he fell into an open manhole.

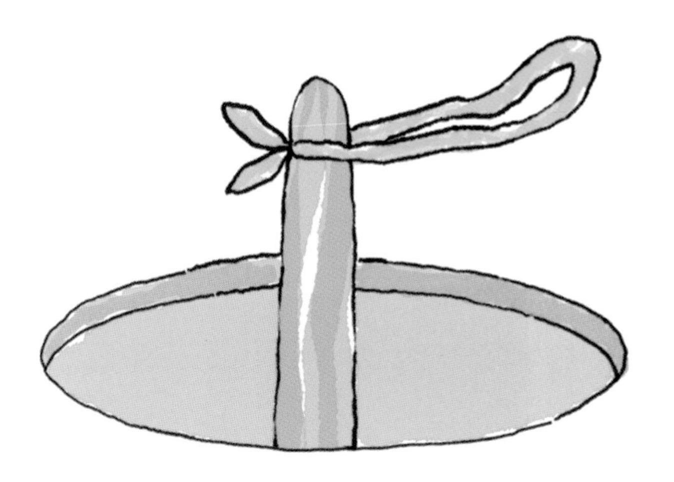

"Someone please help me!" cried Monsieur Saguette.

"Hold onto my hand and I'll pull you up," offered a passing construction worker.

But even when he stood on tiptoe Monsieur Saguette could not reach the worker's hand.

And the sewer was beginning to flood ...

"Quick, grab onto my baguette," said Monsieur Saguette, and the worker pulled him out of the manhole just in time.

"Thank you," said Monsieur Saguette.

"You're welcome," said the worker.

"Gurgle gurgle," said the sewer.

At last Monsieur Saguette arrived home.

"Ah! Soup and bread!" he said, smacking his lips. "My favorite!"

After his delicious lunch Monsieur Saguette shook the crumbs from his tablecloth out the window.

"Now you too can enjoy my baguette," he said to the birds on the street. "Bon appétit!"

And the birds replied, "Tweet! Tweet!"